PETE PIG CLEANS UP

First Steck-Vaughn Edition 1992

Copyright © 1989 American Teacher Publications

Published by Steck-Vaughn Company

Library of Congress number: 89-3541

Library of Congress Cataloging in Publication Data.

Hulbert, Jay.
  Pete Pig cleans up / Jay Hulbert; illustrated by John Killgrew.

  (Real readers)
  Summary: Peter Pig finds some surprising things when he starts to clean up his room.
  [1. Pigs—Fiction. 2. Cleanliness—Fiction. 3. Orderliness—Fiction.] I. Karas, Brian, ill. II. Title. III. Series.
PZ8.3.H876Pe   1989   [E]—dc19   89-3541

ISBN 0-8172-3504-3   hardcover library binding

ISBN 0-8114-6703-1   softcover binding

  3 4 5 6 7 8 9 0   96 95 94 93 92

PETE PIG CLEANS UP

by Jay Hulbert
illustrated by John Killgrew

STECK-VAUGHN
C O M P A N Y
A Subsidiary of National Education Corporation

A pig named Pete
Looked at his home,
Looked at his home and said,
"This is a mess!
In this big mess
I can not find my bed!"

4

"This day I will
Pick up my mess
And clean!" said Pete the pig.
He picked a spot
Down in the mess,
And there Pete Pig did dig.

He found his drum,
His bike, his duck.
He found his doll named Matt.
He dug deep, deep
Down in a pile—
And there he found his cat!

"Oh look!" said Pete,
"I found my book!
I like this book!" he said.
"It tells the tale
of Little Bear!"
And Pete sat down and read.

Pete read the book
And tossed it down,
And found his big red cup.
He dug up games
And robes and kites,
His piles piled up and UP!

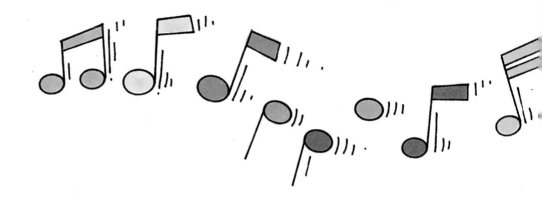

He beat his drum,
"I want to play
And sing!" said Pete the pig.
And sing he did,
Up on a crate,
And did a happy jig.

Pete Pig jumped down
And found his truck.
He had to stop and play.
He piled up hills
In all his mess,
And played for all the day.

16

"Yum, yum!" Pete said,
"Now, time to eat!"
He ate a happy meal.
He ate a big, ripe
Orange, and he
Tossed down all the peel.

"My home is still
A mess!" Pete said.
"And I have cleaned all day!
What can I do?
I clean, but still
It will not go away!"

"My bed!" Pete yelled.
"I found my bed!"
And BOOM he gave a leap.
With all his messes
Still a mess,
Pete Pig fell fast asleep!

Sharing the Joy of Reading

Beginning readers enjoy reading books on their own. Reading a book is a worthwhile activity in and of itself for a young reader. However, a child's reading can be even more rewarding if it is shared. This sharing can enhance your child's appreciation—both of the book and of his or her own abilities.

Now that your child has read **Pete Pig Cleans Up**, you can help extend your child's reading experience by encouraging him or her to:

- Retell the story or key concepts presented in this story in his or her own words. The retelling can be oral or written.

- Create a picture of a favorite character, event, or concept from this book.

- Express his or her own ideas and feelings about the characters in this book and other things the characters might do.

Here is an activity you can do together to help extend your child's appreciation of this book. You and your child might want to find some other funny rhymes, either story length, or simple short rhymes. Together you might reread favorite rhymes from books you have at home or find new rhymes to share in books in your local library.